African Stories

Retold by Robert Hull
Illustrated by Peter Kettle

Wayland

Tales From Around The World

African Stories
Egyptian Stories
Greek Stories
Native North American Stories
Roman Stories
Viking Stories

Editor: Catherine Ellis
Series Designer: Tracey Cottington
Book Designer: Derek Lee
Map on page 47 by Peter Bull

First published in 1992 by
Wayland (Publishers) Ltd
61 Western Road, Hove
East Sussex BN3 1JD, England

British Library Cataloguing in Publication Data
Hull, Robert
African Stories. – (Tales from Around
the World Series)
I. Title II. Kettle, Peter III. Series
398.2096

ISBN 0-7502-0338-2

Typeset by Dorchester Typesetting Group Ltd
Printed in Italy by G. Canale & C.S.p.A., Turin
Bound in France by A.G.M.

Contents

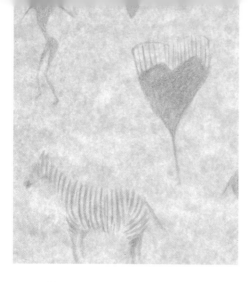

Introduction

*A*frica is where you come from. Not personally of course, unless you were born there, but because that is where the first people lived. From there, over millions of years, humans spread round the earth, taking on slightly different features and colours in icy regions, hot dry areas and wet forests, living and learning about the earth until the human race finally arrived at – you.

That is one reason for taking an interest in Africa. Another is that Africa is such a large part of the earth. Think of the biggest countries in the world – Australia, Brazil, Canada, China and the USA for instance. Imagine all those countries, and then all the other land in the world. Africa is about one fifth of it, which is a hugeness that is quite hard to grasp!

Africa is made up of many countries and many peoples with different ways of life. They all have their own histories and traditions. Today, most Africans live by different sorts of farming, but there are also wandering nomadic peoples, peoples of the thick tropical forest, peoples who look after cattle on the savannah and city dwellers.

Africa has more than a thousand different languages. In Zaire alone there are more than three hundred. Some languages, like Yoruba in Nigeria, are spoken by millions of people, but there are perhaps fewer than a hundred people left who speak the language of the San in Namibia. Some languages are spoken over a large area, like Arabic, which is used from Egypt across to Morocco, and Swahili, which is widely used in East Africa.

There are many different religions too. Countries in the north of Africa are mainly Muslim; much of the rest of Africa is Christian, but in other places the older African religions and beliefs still exist.

Although there are these big differences and huge distances, some things do unite Africa. All over Africa there has always been music and poetry and story-telling. Outside the towns of Africa there is often no electricity, and the tropical sun sets early. The evening is the time for singing, listening to poems, telling stories.

Story-tellers are very important people. They have to know many things – the history of their people, their customs and religion, the habits of animals, the ways of plants and trees, the behaviour of ghosts. Story-tellers must know about all kinds of strange and remarkable events, but also about ordinary life and what real people are like. Sometimes the people in the stories are disguised as animals.

There are hundreds and hundreds of African stories about living creatures. Some creatures, like Anansi the Spider, Chameleon, Hare, Tortoise and Elephant, have many stories told about them. They are the creatures who have been close to the daily lives of Africans for centuries. In many stories about the creation of the world, animals are the first 'people'. Later, when human beings came, they and the animal people could understand each others' language.

The stories in this book are written down in English, so that you can share them, but only a few years ago one or two of them weren't written down in any language. A book on my desk has Somali in one half of the book and English in the other. The Somali half looks like this: *Sheekoxariiooyin Soomaliyeed* (meaning 'Somali Folk Tales'), and off the story goes – *'Waxaa la yiri waagii hore cirka … '* ('In the beginning of time … '). I can imagine those strange – for me – words in that language I can't understand being spoken round a fire hundreds of years ago, and being spoken now. Can you imagine a million other stories being told round other fires, in a thousand other languages? Here are just some of them.

5

A Holy Cat

Animals appear in hundreds of African stories. Sometimes, as in this story from North Africa, they are human beings in disguise.

A cat goes on a pilgrimage

A well-known cat from a certain alley in a town in North Africa decided to go on a pilgrimage to the Holy City. When he told the other cats about his unusual plan there was so much talk about it down the alleyways and on the street corners that the rats and mice heard about it too. They all wondered what the cat was thinking of.

When the cat came back after his journey he was quite changed, and went round being very religious. He wore a white turban and a white flowing burnous, just like any other Muslim scholar, and instead of stalking rats and mice he would stand on his favourite street corner praying and reading. Sometimes he would walk round with his eyes half-closed and his nose in the air, with his mind obviously on higher things.

The rats were puzzled, and to find out what was going on the chief rat went to pay the cat his compliments and hope he had a good pilgrimage. When the chief rat arrived the cat had a pair of reading glasses on, and was reading the Holy Book.

The rat bowed. 'Good morning, reverend cat. I have been sent by the rodent community to pay our respects to your learned reverence, and to ask what wisdom you wish to impart to us from your trip to the Holy Place.'

'Welcome, rodent chief. Yes, I have learned much at the Holy City. I have learned to read and pray. I have learned to love my fellow-creatures and respect their freedom. I have learned that it is wicked to kill rats and mice and eat them. I used to hunt them for food, and sometimes I even enjoyed it, but this unfortunate habit of mine is a thing of the past. You rats and mice may run and frolic wherever you will. In my new holy life I eat only dates and milk and bread.'

The rat bowed again and hurried back to tell the others the news. They weren't sure how to take it, but decided they would watch and see if they could observe any of these changes for themselves.

Next morning two of them were having a quiet sip at a gutter when they saw the cat coming down the alley towards them, walking very slowly, with his head in the air. He didn't seem to see the rats at all.

He was reading in the Holy Book, learning bits from it, muttering the words over and over to himself. Then he stopped and took out a piece of bread from his burnous, and stood there nibbling it for a minute or two, before he went on.

The same thing happened the next day to some other rats further down the street. Then to some mice. And again the day after to another pair of rats. Gradually all the rats and mice became convinced that the cat had really changed its ways and was trying to be a genuine holy cat. They got used to him walking by reading, taking no notice of them.

Finally the rats and mice lost all their terror of the cat. One day two rats saw him coming down the street, and because they had no fear of him any more, carried on nibbling at a bit of bread that someone had dropped. These two rats happened to be the two plump female rats that the holy cat, before he had been on his pilgrimage, especially used to fancy. In the days before he became saintly, he'd been fond of crouching down with his head on his paws gazing at their rat-holes in the wall, occasionally twitching the sides of his mouth in sheer longing. But the plump female rats had been too wily, and the cat had never got near either of them.

On this particular morning, though, they carried on quietly nibbling. They knew that since his pilgrimage the cat no longer hunted, but lived on dates and plain bread and devoted his life to holiness and sacred things.

And so the cat came walking slowly by, muttering words from his Holy Book. If you'd been looking hard at him you'd have seen a tiny tremble of mouth and a twitch of whisker just before he – aaarrgh! – pounced! He grabbed them both in his mouth and trotted off round the corner.

A very unholy act for a holy cat!

The rats and mice forgot something rats and mice should always remember – that a cat that has been on a pilgrimage and reads holy books is still a cat.

10

Two Sisters

*I*n the north-east part of Somalia, children often don't go to bed until late in the evening, after the animals have been milked. Then they sit round the fire and listen to a story-teller tell all kinds of stories. Some will be about situations which they might meet in later life, such as the kind of person it might be best to marry.

A question of marriage

There once lived two sisters. One was extremely beautiful but not very intelligent, and the other was very intelligent but not at all beautiful.

A young man came to the village looking for a wife. He spoke to the girls' father and asked permission to speak to them about marriage. From talking to the father he learned about the daughters. Then he went over to talk to them. The beautiful one dazzled him with her shining eyes and hair. She was so beautiful he could hardly think. He just gazed at her, saying hardly anything.

After a while he managed to pull his eyes away from her to talk to her sister. She didn't have the same effect on him, but her voice was quiet and he found himself listening to every word. He left, promising to return in a few days.

He didn't know what to do. In his imagination he saw the beautiful sister looking at him with her

11

glistening eyes and smile. He just couldn't stop seeing her eyes and her smile.

Then he remembered the quiet way the other sister had spoken, and found he kept remembering things she had said. He realized he had forgotten everything the beautiful one had said. He wondered why.

A few days passed, and the young man was still confused. He decided to go and see the wise man, Kabacalaf. Perhaps he would have some good advice. So off he went and told Kabacalaf about the two sisters.

Kabacalaf listened to the young man very carefully, and sat thinking for a few minutes. Then he said, 'I have thought of a way you can be sure to choose the sister you will be happiest with. You must ask each sister three questions. The first is, "What do men need for a bedspread?" The second question is, "What is a camel's pen?" And the last question you must ask them is, "What is the best sauce for millet?" Ask both sisters these questions and you will know who to ask to marry.'

The young man was puzzled. 'How will I know?'

'By their answers,' Kabacalaf said.

'But what are ... ' the young man started to say. Kabacalaf held up his hand. 'You will know.'

The young man had to be satisfied with that, so off he went, thinking how all wise men liked complicated mysteries. He still didn't know how he would know who to marry, because Kabacalaf hadn't told him the answers. They were such obvious, easy questions there must be riddling answers. Or perhaps not? He was almost as confused as before.

The day came when he was due to go back to the two sisters. He went first to the father and asked if he could talk again to both sisters and ask them each three questions. The father agreed, but was a bit puzzled.

So the young man asked the two sisters the three questions. Their replies were very different.

The beautiful one said, 'Those are easy questions! For a bedspread men need a mat of fibre and grass. A camel's pen is a high fence to keep them in at night. And the best sauce for a meal of millet is ghee and milk. There!'

But her sister had quite different things to say. 'Men's bedspread is peace. If men have peace they will sleep – wherever they are. The camel's pen is man, because it is man who looks after the camels and herds them together for safety. And the best sauce for a meal of millet is hunger. Without hunger no meal of millet gives its best flavour.'

Listening to the two sisters, the young man knew whose words he would remember, and whose thoughts went deep. He knew who Kabacalaf thought he should marry.

So he asked her to marry him, and she agreed. He was overjoyed. He knew that he would have the protection of her thoughtfulness. It would be like a roof for their marriage.

13

Chameleon and Hare

*T*he Khoi-khoi people have a story about an insect and a hare taking different messages about death to the first people. This story is also from southern Africa, but the messengers this time are Hare and Chameleon, or Mr Tread-Carefully, as he is sometimes called.

God's message to the first people

Chameleon is wise. He treads carefully, gripping twigs firmly, looking where he places his feet. Even on his longest journeys, he does not hurry. He stops to nibble leaves. He waits silently and looks about him before moving off. He is slow, but sure.

Wherever he goes, Chameleon concentrates so hard that he makes himself look like that place! On a rock he is grey, in a tree he is green. Sometimes he is multi-coloured. That's why Chameleon is a good visitor. When he is with you he can be like you are. He can change and seem to be another person. That way he understands many different things.

This is why, when the world was new, God chose Chameleon to take an important message to the first people on the earth. He knew Chameleon would understand the message, and not forget it. He knew that though Chameleon would take his time, he would

14

go in the right direction and find the first people.

The message was very important: 'People shall not die. When they have finished their time on earth, they shall go away, and then return from time to time, like the moon.'

Chameleon studied the message and memorized it slowly, in his usual careful way, and then he set off to find the first people. It would be a long journey, and he had to conserve his energy, so he stopped frequently to nibble shoots and leaves. Because he hadn't walked along the earth before, he had to keep studying the stars and the shadows of the sun and moon to check he was going the right way.

Along he went steadily, over burning sand and rock and cool river-mud, through soaking jungle and tall dry grass, always watching where he placed his feet. God's message was important, and Chameleon must deliver it without any mishap along the way. Concentrating hard as he walked, he changed into the different colours of the places he passed through. He became yellow with the desert sand, mottled and dark with the shadow on the floor of the jungle, then grey with the hard rock.

Days and days passed. God was beginning to worry. It had been a long time since Chameleon left. What could have happened? Had he lost the way? God thought he would send another messenger, just to make sure the message got through. So he called Hare, the cleverest of the animals, to come to him. He told Hare what had happened. Perhaps Chameleon had lost his way, or fallen off the earth somehow. Hare would have to go and take the same message, in case the people hadn't received it.

God spoke the message very clearly and slowly. Hare said it over once, then again. '"People shall not die. When they have finished their time on earth, they shall go away, and then return from time to time, like the moon." There, I've learned it by heart already,' Hare said. It was exciting work and he wanted to be off. Without another word he raced down towards earth at top speed.

Unlike Chameleon, Hare was there in no time. Soon he was running through the wet grass of the world, tearing this way and that in sheer fun.

He would stop for a second and twiddle his ears, to check on the right direction, then he was off again. He was enjoying his run more than anything he'd ever done. He was full of amazement at all the things he was seeing and doing on earth, and thinking excitedly of the people he would meet.

Hare raced past Chameleon just a little way before he found the first people, but he didn't see him, because he was in an impetuous dash to get to the people's village before night. And suddenly, there Hare was, standing on his hind legs among the people, with an important message from God. 'Now, what was it?' he thought to himself. 'Ah yes, about returning to earth.'

Speaking loudly, Hare gave the message: 'People shall die. When they finish their time here on earth, they shall go away, and not return.' It was not God's message, but Hare brought the words from God and once they were spoken they could not be altered.

Hare stayed with the first people for a while, then hurried off to look round the rest of the earth. When Chameleon arrived, it was too late. It had already been decided that people should die and never return to earth. All the people knew.

Chameleon could not change the way the world was. Instead, he decided to stay with the people and try to share his wisdom with them. He would teach them to concentrate on where they were on earth and to think about how they went along. He would help them to tread carefully on all their paths through the world.

Ata-okolo-inona

Madagascar is an island off the south-east coast of Africa. It is nearly two and a half times the size of the UK. The Malagasy people, who live there, have their own version of the creation of human beings. This story comes from the south-west of the island, where there's very little rain.

Creation of death and rain

Soon after the beginning of time, the Great Spirit, Ndrian-ana-hary, decided to send his son Ata-okolo-inona down to the earth. The Great Spirit told his son to look round the earth and see what it was like, then report back to his father in the sky. If earth seemed a good place for living things, Ndrian-ana-hary would create them. If it didn't, he wouldn't. The plan seemed a sensible one, but plans don't always work out as they should, even when the Great Spirit thinks them up.

Ata-okolo-inona came down to the earth and looked around. At first, especially in the early morning, he liked it. He watched the stars fade away and the brilliant sun come up over the mountain tops. Later he saw the mists disappearing, and then the ocean glittering in the distance. Earth was beautiful, he decided, a good place for living.

As he walked down from the mountains, he could imagine how well living things would fit in. In his mind's eye he could see huge trees growing on the steep slopes. He saw animals resting in the shade underneath them, and other creatures climbing in the leafy branches. He thought how some beings could live in the depth of the ocean, and others could ride on the waves. Some could move about in the air, where there was plenty of room.

But as the morning wore on, and the sun rose higher and higher, Ata-okolo-inona began to feel uncomfortable. Earth was much hotter than the cool sky. There was only one small river, and a lake that glinted in the sun. He could hardly look at it without seeing creatures drinking there, but the rest of the earth seemed dry.

As the days passed and the sun came back from the south end of the world, the air grew even hotter. Ata-okolo-inona walked away to the north to keep cooler, but the sun climbed higher in the sky each day. It soon became so hot it was impossible for him to stay on the surface of the earth, under the beating sun. To escape from the glare and heat, Ata-okolo-inona dug down into the earth. It was beautifully cool there, so there he stayed.

His father, Ndrian-ana-hary, waited for his son for many years. He was patient. He knew that it would take a long time to walk round the earth and decide whether there should be creatures living on it. Ata-okolo-inona would need to search for good places, he thought, and imagine what kind of creatures would be suited to living there.

But Ata-okolo-inona didn't come back, even after a hundred years, and Ndrian-ana-hary decided that his son must be lost. All he could do was send some servants down to earth to look for him. He could not go down himself, because there was no one else to look after the sky and the stars, and to make sure the sun and moon rose at the right times, and that the winds and tides kept moving. Ndrian-ana-hary had never shared with anyone the secrets of running the world. So it had to be his servants who went to look for Ata-okolo-inona.

These servants were the first men and women. They wandered in all directions to find the Great Spirit's lost son, but there was no sign of him. He had vanished.

The servants wandered all over the world. They were on earth just to find Ata-okolo-inona, and they couldn't. Their lives were without happiness. The earth was so hot and its surface so bare they could hardly exist. Nothing grew in the harsh, dry soil, and they had no animals. It seemed pointless to stay.

The servants met together and decided that one of them should return to the sky. They had to tell Ndrian-ana-hary that they had failed, and they wanted to know what to do next. So one of the servants went off up into the sky, and the others waited behind on earth. They waited and waited, but the servant didn't return.

So another servant was sent, then another, and then another. None of them returned. They needed help, and advice, but Ndrian-ana-hary didn't send any of them back with instructions about what to do.

The servants who were sent to Ndrian-ana-hary were the first Dead.

And this is why men and women die. They are still sent from earth to their creator, Ndrian-ana-hary, to find out what they should do. None of them has ever come back, so the men and women on earth are confused, and never know exactly what to do, because they still cannot find Ata-okolo-inona. Should they give up the search or go on looking? Where should they look? They have looked everywhere, but they return to the same places, in case Ata-okolo-inona should appear.

Ndrian-ana-hary wanted men and women to stay on earth, so he decided to make earth a better place to live. He created rain and sent it falling to earth; it would make earth a better place. His servants could live there and grow crops and have children. There would be some hope of happiness for them. And if there was rain there would be many rivers, not just one small one, and lakes, and many creatures could come and drink from them.

So now the earth is cooler, and men and women can live on it happily. Now there are often bursts of rain over the forests to soak the ferns and fill up the streams again. Now there are cattle to drink at the pools and water-holes, and their reflections stretch over the water. All this, so that men and women could carry on searching for the lost Ata-okolo-inona.

24

The Kid Goat

A story from Ethiopia about the case of the injured kid goat, and how the judge came to his decision.

It was nearly midday, and the girl had been watching her father's goats since early morning. To escape the heat she decided she would rest for a while in the shade of a tree. She didn't mean to fall asleep, but after a while her eyes became heavy and she couldn't stay awake. She had a dream about swimming in a cool river, and as she was climbing out of the water she woke up.

She looked round her with a start. She began to count her flock and soon realized that some of the young kids had disappeared. They must have wandered off. She jumped up and went running this way and that to try to find them. They were not behind the bushes, they were not on the other side of the little hill, they were not down by the stream. Had they gone off along the road? Were they lost? What would her father say?

She ran back along the road that led to her village. There was a man sitting by the roadside brewing up a cup of coffee. She would ask him if he had seen them.

'Excuse me, have you seen any of my little goats running along the road?' she said.

The man looked up and saw the girl speaking to him. He only saw her. He was deaf, and couldn't hear a word. But he was used to people stopping and waving their arms, indicating they wanted to know the

way to the water-hole, so he thought the girl was asking the same question. He pointed towards the river, and told her, 'over there'.

'Oh, thank you,' she said, and ran off under the trees towards the river.

As it happened, and it was a complete coincidence, her little goats had wandered to the river. There they were, nibbling grass at the water's edge. She was overjoyed. But then she saw that one of them had hurt its foot and couldn't move. It must have slipped and injured itself among the rocks that led down to the river. She lifted the kid in her arms and started back, calling the others to follow.

On the way back she passed the old man at the edge of the road again. She felt grateful to him, and also a bit sorry for him. He seemed to be sitting there on his own with nothing to do. Perhaps he would like to have the injured kid to look after. Her father would understand. The girl spoke to him. 'As you see, I found them. Thank you for helping me. Would you like to have this young kid to look after?' And she held out the kid with the injured foot.

The old man couldn't hear her, of course, and he thought she was holding out the kid for him to see the injury that had been done. She seemed to be accusing him. He was polite to her, but quite angry at the thought.

'No, it wasn't me. It was nothing to do with me,' he said.

She was puzzled. Surely he would like to hold the kid. 'But you showed me the way,' she said.

'It happens *every* day around here,' he told her crossly, remembering all the people who asked him the way to the river. He could see that the girl still believed it was him.

'They were just where you said!' she said, feeling even more confused.

'I tell you it was not me. I am not responsible!' He was shouting now, and the young goatherd really couldn't understand why. Perhaps he just couldn't be bothered to look after an injured kid. How strange and ungrateful of him to refuse her offer!

As they were arguing, some people came round a

28

corner in the road and heard the raised voices. A man asked what the argument was about.

'I had lost some of my young goats and this man said they were down by the river. I offered him this kid as a reward for his help, but he just got angry.' As she spoke she lifted the kid towards the old man, showing how she offered it to him.

At this the deaf man stepped towards her with a shout, 'Do not insult me!' He was waving his arms about violently. 'It was nothing to do with me, do you hear. I have said so! Don't you people believe me?' And as he swung round to the others one of his waving arms hit the girl's arm and she lost her hold on the kid. It squirmed about in alarm and fell to the ground.

'Look what you have done,' she cried. 'You hit me on the arm! I shall tell the judge. You saw him! I shall take him to the judge. He hit me!'

The people watching agreed and nodded their heads. 'Yes, yes. He did! He did!'

Of course, the old man hadn't meant to hit her, on the arm or anywhere, but he realized it looked as if he had. That was serious. And there were witnesses. But he felt he was in the right, and was sure he would be able to persuade the judge that he was not responsible for the injury to the young kid. So off they went down the road to find the judge. They made a strange group: the bewildered girl, the deaf man, the ignorant spectators, and the happily bleating goats that were the cause of it all.

They soon came to the village and went to the judge's house. He had been having a sleep, and when he came out to listen to their stories he was still yawning and stretching his arms. The girl told her story first, then the man told his, and lastly the spectators gave their account of what had happened.

Now all this excitement had taken place in quite a short time, and it was still the hottest part of the day. The judge hadn't woken up properly from his afternoon sleep, and he was finding all the stories rather difficult to follow. The goats hadn't stopped bleating for a second, which didn't help his

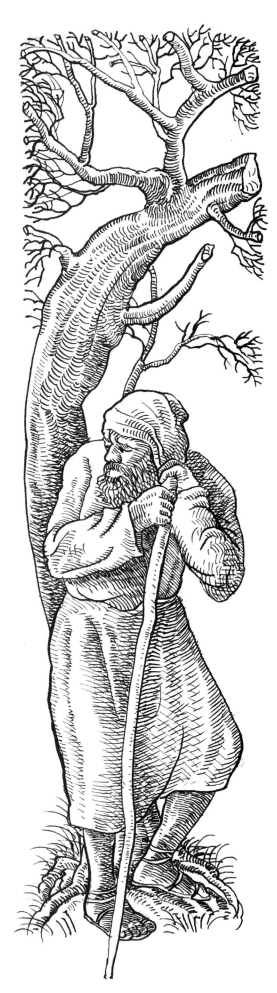

29

concentration, so he missed some of what people said. He was also very short-sighted, and hadn't been able to find his glasses when he was woken up. He didn't like to mention any of these things of course, because he was a very well-known judge who had been appointed by the chief of the people a long time ago.

He was also a very successful judge, the reason being that most of the quarrels he had to settle were very similar. Most of them were family squabbles about things like husbands not treating their wives properly, or sons and daughters not showing enough respect to their elders.

When he had heard enough of the girl, and the deaf man and the spectators, he put his hand up to stop the talk. 'Listen to my judgement,' he said. 'These family quarrels are an insult to our great Chief. They must cease. Therefore, listen.'

He spoke to the spectators first. 'You must learn to leave husband and wife to settle their own quarrels and not make them worse by interfering.'

Then he turned to the old man. 'From this moment you must stop mistreating your wife.'

Next he turned to the girl, who was still carrying the young goat. 'As for you, you must learn not to be late with your husband's meals.'

And then he peered forward, blinking, at the young kid. 'And finally, may this beautiful baby live long and bring great joy to both of you. May it teach you the need for peace and harmony, so that you never quarrel again.'

The Severed Head

The merchant and the head

*T*his story comes from West Africa, though versions of it, with different characters, are told in other parts of Africa.

One day, many years ago, a merchant was travelling through the forest when ahead of him on the path he saw a freshly cut tree-stump with something perched on top of it. From a distance he couldn't tell what it was, then as he drew closer he suddenly recognized – ugh! – a severed head! He stopped to look at the grisly sight. Perhaps it was the cruelty of a mad king. Perhaps it was murder, or the work of a robber.

'I wonder what happened to you?' he said aloud.

'Don't say anything,' came a voice.

The traveller went cold. It couldn't be, but it was. A reply. It was the head speaking. The head had used words. The traveller stared at its closed lips.

'Don't say anything.'

Again. This time the traveller watched the mouth open and close. He shuddered and ran.

He ran wildly for a mile or so, then had to slow down to a walk. His heart was thumping too fast and he was out of breath and scared stiff – a severed head had spoken to him. On he went, his mind in a turmoil about what he had just seen and heard. Was it a piece of spirit trickery? Had the dead started to talk?

Soon he came to a very large town. He had to tell someone, and since it was an important matter if the dead had started talking, he asked the way to the king's palace. There were soldiers on guard with long spears and big knives. The merchant said he had some very important news for the king, which he must give him at once. He was taken to a room where the king was meeting with all the other chiefs. 'This man says he has urgent news for the king,' the guard said.

'Yes? Well, what is this urgent message? I and my chiefs are discussing important things.' The king sounded stern, but the merchant knew that his news was so important and amazing the king would forgive him for interrupting.

'Your Majesty, an hour ago, while I was travelling this way through the forest, I passed a man's severed head, placed on a tree-trunk.' The merchant swallowed, looking round at the chiefs.

'And that is what you have kindly interrupted us to say?' the king asked. He was smiling, in a cold-looking way, as if he thought the merchant was a bit mad.

'It was not that, your Majesty. The severed head spoke to me.' The merchant paused again, feeling nervous. Surely the king would realize it could be an important message, that the head had something important to say.

'A talking head? On a tree-stump? A head that happens to be dead? How interesting! Where can we find this fascinating tree-stump?'

'I promise you, your Majesty. Let me give all my goods to your Majesty's subjects if I am not telling the truth. Perhaps the dead have started speaking to the living. Surely someone could come with me to listen to it speak, and prove that I am not lying.' The poor merchant looked anxious.

It was easier for the king to send someone with the merchant than to waste time talking, so he said, 'Very well. Some of my guards shall go with you to see if you're telling the truth. If you are, you shall be rewarded. If not, you shall lose your own head at the same spot. Guards, away with him!'

So off they went back into the forest, the merchant leading the way. After about an hour's walk, he recognized the clearing where the tree-stump was, and, sure enough, there was the severed head. 'See, over there,' he said to the guards, and across they went to the tree-stump.

The traveller started talking to the head. 'These men have come to hear you speak. The king does not believe me, and when you reply to me as you did before, we shall go back to the palace and the king will know I was telling the truth. So, will you please tell them that you spoke to me before?'

He stopped, and waited. Silence.

'It is important that you speak. Say anything. It doesn't matter what you say, just speak, oh head, I beg you.'

Silence. The merchant stared at the head. It seemed to have an echo of a smile on its face, a smile like the king's cold smile. The merchant then realized that the severed head was not going to say anything. He turned round to look at the guards.

It was obvious to the guards that the merchant had been lying, trying to impress the king. Their orders were to behead the merchant on the spot if he was lying and wasting their time – which he clearly was. So the guards carried out their orders, and the man's severed head rolled in the dust. As the guards stared down at the foolish merchant's head, from behind them came, 'I told him not to say anything.'

They froze, and then turned. It was the head on the tree-trunk. 'I told him. I said, "Don't say anything."' The guards ran, and ran, and ran.

Half an hour later they pulled up for breath. They couldn't believe what they had heard, but they had heard it.

Should they tell the king?

35

Nogwaja

S tories about the exploits of the rascal Hare are told in many parts of Africa. He has many different names. In Zulu stories Hare is called Nogwaja the Mischief Maker, and this story is about how he gained his cunning.

How Nogwaja gained his cunning

Nogwaja the Hare, the Mischief Maker, wasn't always as cunning as he is now. He has always enjoyed playing tricks on people, but at first they sometimes weren't clever enough, and went wrong. This is the story of how he gained his real cunning.

Long ago there was a great drought. All the water-holes on earth dried up except one – Elephant's. She and her family still had clear cool water to drink and splash in and squirt over themselves. The other animals watched enviously, but the most envious of all was Nogwaja. As he watched, he grew thirstier and dustier and crosser every minute.

Nogwaja was determined to think up a plan to trick Elephant and get her water. He thought and thought and thought. Suddenly, he had it! He would make use of

Honeyguide. He knew that Honeyguide had honey to drink, but that she was still thirsty because, like the rest of the animals, she had no water.

For his plan to trick Elephant, Nogwaja had to get some honey. To do that, he needed something to carry the honey in, so he crept into First Woman's hut while she was out, and stole a calabash. Then he went to Honeyguide, and said, 'If you let me have some of your honey I'll let you have beautiful clear water from my water-hole.'

Being thirsty, Honeyguide agreed, and Nogwaja went with her to the bees' nest where Honeyguide poured Nogwaja a whole calabash full of clear yellow delicious honey. Nogwaja told Honeyguide to meet him the next day by the wait-a-minute tree, then off he went to find Elephant.

'Elephant,' he said, 'I have brought you a gift of the most beautiful clear yellow water from my water-hole.'

Elephant tasted it. Mmmm. Delicious. She immediately wanted more.

'Nogwaja the Hare, it's the most beautiful, sweet water I've ever tasted. Where is this water-hole? I would like to share it. Can I share it?'

Nogwaja, being very cunning, put on a serious, doubtful look. 'It's a long way, Elephant, over the hills, at least a day's walk.' He knew that if he made it sound difficult to get there Elephant would be even keener to go. 'I will tell you the way if you like. But while you're away drinking at my water-hole shall I look after yours and use it myself till you come back?'

'Of course,' said Elephant, who was eager to have this new water-hole for her family. So off went Elephant and her family towards the hills and the new water-hole.

Nogwaja had told Honeyguide to meet him next day at the wait-a-minute tree if she wanted to have some water to drink. But Nogwaja preferred to keep Elephant's water-hole to himself. He wasn't going to share this precious water with stupid old Honeyguide.

Honeyguide waited at the wait-a-minute tree for a long time, and when Nogwaja didn't come she began to suspect she'd been tricked. She flew high in the air and far down below her keen eyes saw Nogwaja drinking at Elephant's water-hole. Down she flew, but Nogwaja shooed her away. 'There is not enough water for two. Off you go.' So Honeyguide had to go back the way she came.

In the meantime, Elephant and her family had been walking all day and still hadn't come to Nogwaja's water-hole. On her way back home Honeyguide saw them and flew down to tell them about Nogwaja's trickery.

'Elephant, Nogwaja has been up to his tricks again. All you will find here is wild honey, which you thought was clear yellow water. The bees will fight and sting you to stop your large trunk stealing into their hives. And even if you drink you will still be thirsty afterwards and need water.' Elephant couldn't believe her ears. She was furious. She trumpeted and stamped. She and her family started back across the hills.

Early next morning Elephant and her family reached their water-hole again. Elephant found Nogwaja resting in the grass. She caught him in her trunk, lifted him up

high and whirled him till he was sick and dizzy. Then, with a final whisk of her trunk, she threw him away into the long grass, and stood there still trumpeting with fury.

After that, the other animals began to avoid Nogwaja the Not-So-Clever-After-All. It wasn't wise to be friendly with an animal that Elephant was angry with. Soon no one would talk to Nogwaja or sit and eat with him. He began to live a lonely life, and as sometimes happens to lonely creatures he became bitter. 'Why should I suffer so much more than anyone else, just because I played a simple clever trick on Elephant? Why should Elephant have so much power and so many friends, while I am ignored by everybody? How can I become powerful and have friends again? Why can't I be king? King Nogwaja!'

He liked the sound of that. Perhaps the others would call him King Nogwaja if he could get more power than Elephant. Now Nogwaja really wanted to get revenge on Elephant. What could he do? Suddenly, he had a brilliant idea. He would ask other First Beings to help him. He was determined to go to all the powerful Beings and ask them for some of their power. Then the creatures who ignored him would have to take notice of him.

So he asked Wind if he would teach him how to push down trees and howl frighteningly. But Wind ignored him. He went on idly riding across the plain and had nothing to say to Nogwaja. He asked River if she could teach him to grow bigger and bigger and swallow up other creatures and sweep them out of his way in a flood. No reply. River went quietly glittering along as though she was half asleep. She had enough trouble to find her way to the sea without stopping to listen to mad hare talk.

Finally, when Sun came close at noon, Nogwaja tried asking how he could learn to dry up water-holes (such as Elephant's, he thought) and dry up the land and make other creatures thirsty and hungry. Sun could see hare was so crazy with bitterness he just wanted to get away from him, so he slid behind a mountain and disappeared for the night.

Nogwaja didn't know what to do. He lay in the long

cool grass, staring up into the darkening trees, wondering what power he could get hold of to make others respect him again. As Nogwaja watched, Moon climbed up out of the wait-a-minute tree, and walked slowly up to the mountain top, and stood there watching the earth. Perhaps he should talk to Moon. But she was far away, high on the mountain top, too high to reach. Unless, unless . . . Perhaps he could learn to leap higher. He would start with leaping over small things, and then try higher ones, and so on, until perhaps one day . . .

Next day Nogwaja set to work. He practised leaping over small rocks, then over small bushes, until soon he could soar over the wait-a-minute tree. He went on practising until finally he thought it was time to leap high up to Moon. He waited until Moon was close to earth again, standing just at the top of the mountain. Nogwaja hurled himself upwards past the trees, the mists, the hills, and even some of the lowest stars that hung in the valleys, until he realized he had found Moon, and was with her there, high in the night.

What did he ask Moon? What did Moon say? We don't know. It was too far away for anyone to hear and tell. But Honeyguide said she saw Nogwaja creep back to earth along the dewy wet track early next morning as Sun came over the mountain again. She saw Nogwaja limping along, shivering a little in his bedraggled fur.

The other creatures noticed a difference in Nogwaja. He played tricks as before, but never got caught as he did when he angered Elephant. Now he could outwit Jackal, and Monkey, and Lion, and Elephant, all of them. And there was another difference – Nogwaja's eyes. In the dark, they shone with Moon's light.

They say that now, every month, Nogwaja visits Moon. Each time Moon comes close and spreads her full light wide over the earth, Nogwaja is there with her, renewing his cunning. If you look hard at Moon when she is near to earth and round, you will see the outline of Nogwaja's shadow. Watch for yourself when Moon next rises. You will be able to see whether Nogwaja is with her, or whether he has already come back to play some cunning tricks on a fellow-creature.

Ghosts

In the Congo, people believe that ghosts who leave the bodies of human beings when they die don't go wandering about aimlessly. They have places to live, as living bodies do.

The hunter and the ghost

A young man was returning from a few days' hunting in the forest. Over his shoulder was slung a dead antelope, and by his side trotted two dogs. The dogs were wondering when they would stop for the night. The hunter was looking for a place to rest. They were all tired, and it was getting dark.

At the side of the track, its outline visible against the rising moon, the hunter saw what looked like a house. He went over to inspect it. The door was swinging open, and creepers hung down across the entrance. He pushed them aside. There was no sign of life. Obviously no one had lived in the house for years. The hunter threw down the antelope carcass and whistled his dogs in. They trotted up to the door, then stopped and whimpered. They didn't want to go in, and the hunter had to go outside and push them across the threshold. He pulled the rickety door closed after them.

The hunter found some wood and made a fire. He cut off some antelope and cooked it. It was delicious. He and his dogs ate their fill, then he hung the remains of the animal by a cord from the ceiling and lay down in front of the fire, watching the shadows flickering against the walls of the hut. He began to turn over in his mind the events of the few days' hunting, but he was totally exhausted and fell asleep in minutes. So did the two dogs; they were weary too, and full of antelope.

The house was still. Outside were the endless night noises of the forest, but inside there was only the clicking of the dying fire, and the wind making uneven breathing sounds along the roof. The hunter and his dogs slept peacefully. Nothing except the loudest din would have woken them. Not even the ghost woke them. There was only a slight whimper from one of the dogs as, half-way through the night, a white glow appeared in the doorway and a skeleton shape half-stepped, half-drifted carefully indoors.

The ghost wasn't visiting. It lived there. It had been living in the house for a few weeks. Sometimes its home was a cave, but it liked to borrow an empty house, one that had belonged to humans and been abandoned.

If the hunter had called in the daytime, he would have found the owner at home. But night was its time for an hour or two's stroll and wander round the forest. Imagine the ghost's surprise and shock when it came back and saw the figure of the hunter and his dogs stretched asleep round the embers of a fire, and the antelope hanging from the ceiling.

The ghost saw the remains of the cooking. Some people think ghosts don't eat and drink, and don't experience hunger. Of course that isn't true. They like animal meat of all kinds, such as antelope, but what they particularly enjoy is human meat. You could even say they're mad for human flesh, to be eaten at night, because all ghosts hunger to regain their own lost human flesh.

So although the ghost was angry that the hunter and his dogs had settled down for the night in his house, it also realized that a desirable meal was waiting. Through eye-sockets as black as the night sky the ghost gazed down at the helpless hunter, until suddenly a shudder of hunger and excitement, and a shivery rustle went from its head along its bones right to its finger-joints, which made a soft clink.

Now ghosts, made of bones, cannot handle objects. They cannot pick up men's spears or knives, and have had to find another way of cutting meat. In the same way that lobsters have one great claw, ghosts grow a huge thumbnail on one hand. It's about a third of a metre long, and quite wide. When it's shaped and sharpened it can be used in the same way as a knife or an axe. This is ghosts' eating implement, their one piece of cutlery. Imagine having a knife as part of your hand. That's what it's like.

Because ghosts can't cook, the thumbnail-knife needs to be heated to cut easily through meat. It needs to be red hot. The ghost crouched down by the dying fire, and laid his knife in the embers. The hunter and his faithful dogs slept on. One of the dogs was whining

quietly, thumping her tail on the ground, dreaming about the pleasures of being out hunting. The other twitched her paws slightly. The hunter was the stillest of the three, too content even to dream.

The ghost had been watching them, and hadn't noticed that its knife had already started to glow. It would soon be ready. It began to smoke strongly, and the smoke and the smell spread round the hut.

Now ghosts have no scent, and can't smell either, so this one didn't realize that a sharp, unpleasant smell of burning had filled the hut. It couldn't have imagined that in both dogs' dreams there was already something burning. Perhaps it was a forest fire, perhaps a house burning. Whatever was on fire in the dogs' dreams, it woke them both, and they were terrified when they saw a glowing skeleton trembling above them, brandishing a red-hot knife.

Only a moment's fear, then fury. It was the ghost's turn to experience terror. The dogs went for it in one bound. The clatter that followed sounded as if they had dived into a pile of pots. One leap demolished the quivering tower of bones and sent them scattering and sliding to all four corners of the hut.

At this point the hunter woke up, and found himself in the middle of wild noise and commotion. As he rubbed his eyes, he wondered what had woken the dogs and where on earth the bones had come from. And he sat there for a while, just staring round the hut, almost as if he'd seen a ghost.

Notes

Ata-okolo-inona   (p. 20-24)
Ata-okolo-inona appears in the Malagasy story of the creation of living things. He is the son of Ndrian-ana-hary, the Great Spirit.

Burnous   (p. 6)
This is a long cloak with a hood which is commonly worn in North Africa by Arab peoples.

Calabash   (p. 37)
A calabash is the hollowed-out shell of a gourd or a pumpkin, used as a bowl for keeping food and other things in.

Chameleon   (p. 14-18)
Chameleons live in nearly all the countries of Africa. Their amazing ability to change colour to match their surroundings has always fascinated story-tellers. They have a reputation for wisdom because they go along so slowly and carefully. Chameleons are also sometimes called Mr Tread-Carefully.

Elephant   (p. 36-41)
In African stories the elephant, because it isn't attacked except by people, is the wise chief who settles arguments among the animals. When the Ashanti find a dead elephant, they give it a chief's burial, as if it were a human chief from the past.

Hare   (p. 14-18, 36-41)
Hare is a character who appears with different names in stories all over Africa. In Zulu stories, like the one in this book, he is called Nogwaja. He is a boasting, cunning trickster who usually gets his own way, although in one story (not in this book) he is beaten in a race by the tortoise.

Honeyguide   (p. 37-38)
Honeyguides are small, brown and grey birds that live in forests. They lead other animals (including people) to wild bees' nests, then after the nests have been plundered they take food for themselves. They eat honey, and also the beeswax, bees and their larvae.

Kabacalaf   (p. 12,13)
Kabacalaf is a young man who appears in many stories from Somalia. Sometimes he is wise and gives advice. His name means 'Owner of Old Shoes'.

Khoi-khoi   (p. 14)
The Khoi-khoi (who used to be known as the Hottentots) live in the Kalahari, in south-west Africa. They are similar to the San. They used to live as nomads, herding animals, hunting and gathering food. But now they have mostly settled.

Moon   (p. 41)
The moon is important in stories and in some religions. In Cameroon the moon-priest can take the moon down and plant her in his garden, as if she were a banana tree. In Namibia hunters blow an antelope horn to greet the moon.

AFRICA

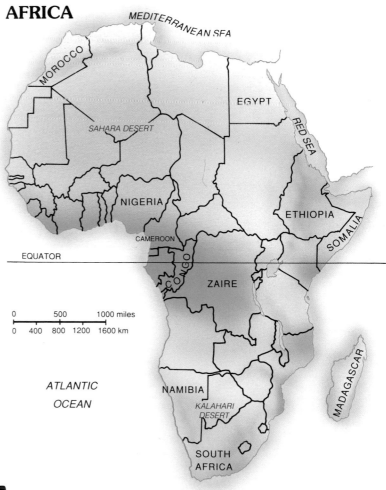

Ndrian-ana-hary   (p. 20-24)
Ndrian-ana-hary is the Great Spirit in the Malagasy story of the creation.

San   (p. 4)
The San (who used to be known as Bushmen) live in small family groups, hunting animals, gathering fruits and roots and sometimes growing vegetables in small gardens. They live in the south-west of Africa, in the Kalahari, and travel about from season to season.

Somalia   (p. 11)
Somalia, the home of the Somali people, is the most easterly country in Africa. Its coastline faces south-east into the Indian Ocean. The Somali people are also scattered through neighbouring parts of Africa. They compose much poetry as well as stories.

Sun   (p. 40)
The sun is important in many African stories. Sometimes it is a god, whom people may visit.

Yoruba   (p. 4)
The Yoruba people live mainly in the south of Nigeria. Their kingdoms and their civilization go back more than a thousand years. They are famous for their poetry and sculpture.

Zulu   (p. 36)
The Zulu people live in the south-east of South Africa. They were scattered tribes until the nineteenth century, when their great leader, Shaka, brought them into one kingdom. Like the Somali and Yoruba peoples, they are well-known for their poetry as well as their stories.

Further Reading

Afrikan Lullaby – Folk Tales from Zimbabwe, Chisiya (Karia Press, 1986)
African Myths and Legends, Kathleen Arnott (Oxford, 1989)
Children of Anansi, Peggy Appiah (Evans, 1985)
Fables from Africa, Jan Knappert (Evans, 1981)
Kings, Gods and Spirits, Jan Knappert (Peter Lowe, 1986)

Tales of an Ashanti Father, Peggy Appiah (Andre Deutsch, 1989)
When Hippo Was Hairy and Other Tales from Africa, Nick Greaves (Lutterworth Press, 1988)
Yoruba Folktales, Amos Tutuola (Ibadan University Press, 1986)